little audrey imaginaut!!

in my pool

little Audrey imaginaut books
by Sheila Cross and Kevin Cook

dadrillio!

A division of Nivek Studios
North Perth, ON, Canada

Text © 2011 by Sheila Cross.
Illustrations and Characters © 2020 Kevin Cook.
Flyleaf Illustrations © 2020 Wilhelm MacGuffin.
Typeset in Aloja Extended; Illustrations rendered
in a variety of creative mediums.
Printed in China.
ISBN 978-1-7774277-0-2 – Hardcover
ISBN 978-1-7774277-1-9 – Paperback
ISBN 978-1-7774277-2-6 – eBook

www.dadrillio.com
@dadrillio
www.nivekstudios.com
@nivekstudios

Design by Nivek Studios.
10 9 8 7 6 5 4 3 2 1
Library of Congress
Cataloging-in-Publication
Data available.

For our little Audrey...
and her snack-size Snoctopus

In the summer I like to play
in the pool in my backyard.

Having fun adventures
isn't very hard.

In my pool I can be
a pirate on a trip,

across the sea to treasured isles
aboard my pirate ship.

In my pool I dance and twirl
   as a lovely mermaid princess,

with braided seagrass for my crown
   and seashells for my dress.

In my pool you must watch out
   for the giant squid,
but I once baked him seaweed cake
   so I'm his favourite kid.

In my pool I ride a raft
    to the land of ice and snow,

and have tea with the polar bears
    on a giant ice flow.

In my pool I crouch my legs
    and blast off from the side,

and zoom through outer space
    on a magic rocket ride.

In my pool I have wings
   and jump from way up high,

I yell "Geronimo"
   as I soar throughout the sky.

In my pool I dive deep
  in a sub made out of cheese,

I explore the caves and canyons
  and go wherever I please.

In my pool I float along
   the surface of the water,

and often I'm joined by my friends
   the dolphin and the otter.

In my pool I blow bubbles
that travel out to sea,

and ask all the seahorses
to come and play with me.

It's always hard to leave the pool
when mom says "Out you get!",

but I know I'll be back tomorrow
getting good and wet.

What adventures happen in your pool?

Lightning Source UK Ltd.
Milton Keynes UK
UKHW050657051220
374638UK00002B/184

9 781777 427702